THE LEGEND OF

Clemens Brentano

Illustrated by Lisbeth Zwerger

Translated by Anthea Bell

A MICHAEL NEUGEBAUER BOOK
NORTH-SOUTH BOOKS / NEW YORK / LONDON

The Duke of Rosery had a very beautiful sister whom he loved more than all the world, and he would do anything to please her. She was extraordinarily fond of flowers, particularly roses, so her brother made almost all his dukedom into one great rose garden. She had another great passion too, for the combing and braiding of her lovely hair. For this purpose she had a number of lady's maids, who were really braiding maids, and who always had golden combs pinned to their dresses.

The princess did nothing all day long but have her hair combed, and then go running about in the garden with her braiding maids until it was untidy again, when they combed it for her once more.

One morning, as she was sitting in the garden with her six maids busy about her, plaiting her six braids of hair, her brother the Duke of Rosery came up to her, leading Prince Evermore by the hand.

"Dear sister," said the Duke, "I have often told you about my dearest friend, Prince Evermore, and you know I have always hoped you would marry him, so that he would stay with me for evermore. Here he is now, and I ask you to give him your heart."

Just at that moment one of the braiding maids pulled at a tangle in Princess Rosalina's hair, which made the Princess very cross, and she cried, "Oh, must you be pulling my hair evermore?"

The maid thought of a clever excuse. "Why, yes, Princess," she said, "it was indeed Prince Evermore who pulled your hair, because the sudden sight of him distracted me."

The Prince was starting to make his own excuses when another of the maids pulled the Princess's hair too, so that Rosalina quite lost her temper, and said to poor Prince Evermore, "Noble Prince, and you too, dear brother, let me tell you that I will no more wed Prince Evermore than a rosebush will marry a pumpkin!" And so saying, she walked away with the braiding maids after her, still plaiting her hair.

The Duke could not offer his friend any comfort. "For she always keeps her word," said he.

"In that case," said Prince Evermore, "I'll be off to seek my fortune."
And he embraced the Duke and went away to see his aunt, Lady
Nevermore, who was a great enchantress, to ask her advice.

One day, several weeks later, Rosalina happened to be walking in the
garden when she saw an old woman looking at all the rosebushes one
by one, shaking her head over each of them. Rosalina went over to her
and asked why she kept shaking her head.

"Because there are so many roses here, yet the loveliest of all is missing,"
said the old woman, — "the monthly rose that flowers for evermore."

"Who owns it?" asked Rosalina. "I must have that rose at any price!"

"Why," said the old woman, "it is yours for the asking!" And she took
the cover off the basket she was carrying, and showed the Princess a
pumpkin with a little rosebush in flower stuck into it. She had put the
rosebush in the pumpkin to keep it fresh.

Rosalina was delighted with the little rosebush, and said, "It is the very
loveliest rosebush I have ever seen, and I must have it for my own. Tell
me what you want for it."

"Two things," said she. "First, I want you to be my guest at my midday
meal, and second, when the rosebush comes into flower once a month,
you and your braiding maids must hold a festival, and you must all jump
over the rosebush. But mind you don't brush off any petals with your
skirts, for none of them must fall to the ground. If one of you does cause
a petal to drop, she must be struck on the hands with rose twigs.

The rosebush itself will give the blows if you speak these words to it:

"LITTLE ROSE,

STRIKE YOUR BLOWS!

STRIKE ME AS YOU WILL,

BECAUSE I JUMPED SO ILL!

I WILL TAKE CHASTISEMENT GLADLY,

ROSE, BECAUSE I JUMPED SO BADLY."

That made the Princess laugh, and she agreed to everything. Then the old woman took a wooden spoon out of her pocket, divided the pumpkin in half with it, took out a spoonful of its seeds and gave them to the Princess to eat. The Princess made a face at first, but when she tried the seeds she thought they tasted delicious, and she ate a good many of them. After that the old woman planted the rosebush under her window, and as it was already bearing a full-blown rose, she said, "Now, Princess Rosalina, call for your braiding maids and hold the first festival of jumping the rose."

So then Rosalina went and told her brother the Duke the whole story, and he summoned drummers and trumpeters and made ready for the festival. When Rosalina and her maids came out, they drew lots to see who was to jump first, and it happened that Rosalina herself was last of all. Most of the girls jumped over the rosebush easily, but the maids who had pulled the Princess's hair while Prince Evermore was asking for her hand in marriage brushed a couple of petals off the rose with the long trains of their dresses, and they had to hold out their hands to the bush, saying:

"LITTLE ROSE,
STRIKE YOUR BLOWS!
STRIKE ME AS YOU WILL,
BECAUSE I JUMPED SO ILL!
I WILL TAKE CHASTISEMENT GLADLY,
ROSE, BECAUSE I JUMPED SO BADLY."

At that, to the amazement of all present, the rosebush struck them on
their fingers a couple of times, so hard that the tears came into their eyes.
When it was Rosalina's turn to jump, she took a good run and she too
would have jumped the rose quite easily, if her braids of hair had not
come undone just as she was jumping and brushed a petal off the rose.
But she caught it as she jumped and swallowed it, before it could fall to
the ground. The whole company clapped and applauded.

Then there was much merriment, with feasting and dancing, and towards
the end of the banquet, when all kinds of toasts were being drunk, the
old woman raised her glass and told Rosalina:

"PETAL AND SEED — YOU'VE EATEN BOTH.
NOW YOU'RE FORCED TO KEEP YOUR OATH!
SINCE ROSE AND PUMPKIN NOW ARE ONE,
WHAT YOU HAVE PROMISED MUST BE DONE.
PRINCE EVERMORE WINS YOUR HAUGHTY HAND!
FAREWELL! I VANISH FROM YOUR LAND."

And with these words, she suddenly vanished away before all eyes. But Rosalina, at whom everyone turned to look, uttered a loud cry and fell down in a faint. She was taken to her room, and she remembered, with great dismay, how she had told the Prince she would have him if rose and pumpkin married.

That night she had very strange dreams. She dreamed that roses were growing out of her mouth, and she had pains in her stomach. Such dreams came to her often, and they grew more and more alarming.

When the little rosebush that bore the monthly roses came into flower again, and she jumped over it once more, she felt melancholy and sick, and she had lost her appetite for food and drink.

At the time of the third festival of the rose, she dreamed she was a pumpkin, and her brother had difficulty in persuading her she was not. But as the fourth festival of the rose approached, she took the idea of being a pumpkin into her head more firmly than ever, and she utterly refused to jump over the rosebush again.

When the fifth festival of the rose came, she could not be induced to leave her room, and she spent all day weeping and wailing because, she said, she turned into a pumpkin. The Duke was much distressed by her delusion, and he called in every doctor in the land, but there was no talking her out of it now.

The sixth festival of the rose came around, and by now the rosebush had grown so large that jumping over it was quite out of the question, all the more so when she was grieving all day long because she was a pumpkin. At the seventh festival of the rose, the rosebush came looking in at her window, by the eighth festival of the rose its branches were growing around her bed, and by the ninth it formed a bower of roses over her. Then she had so vivid a dream that she was a pumpkin, and must die, that she had her brother summoned, and he came into her room with a light. But imagine her surprise next morning when she saw half a great golden pumpkin standing by her bed, with a lovely little girl sleeping in it as if it were a cradle.

Then the Princess was deeply moved. "Ah," she said, "if only good Prince Evermore were here now, I would gladly be his wife!" Then the roses around her bed rustled, and she heard a voice:

A ROSE I DIED, A ROSE I BORE,
A ROSE I LIVE FOR EVERMORE."

At that the Princess was in great distress, realizing that good Prince Evermore had become a rosebush for her sake. She called the little girl Rosepetal, and carried her and the cradle into her own most secret chamber, intending to bring her up there, for she loved the child so much she did not want any other human being to set eyes on her. Rosalina soon became merry again, and she stayed in bed for the next few days and told the braiding maids to plait her hair in a different way, for she used to wear the braids around her head like a wreath, but now she wanted to set a golden cap on it. No sooner had the combing of her hair begun than there came a knock at her door, and they told her the old woman who had brought the pumpkin and the rosebush was outside, wanting to see little Rosepetal. However, the Princess sent back word that the old woman must wait until her hair was combed.

Quarter of an hour later the old woman knocked again, and got the same answer. Another quarter-hour passed, and again she knocked and was told to wait. This happened four times more. The seventh time, the old woman grew very angry and called in through the keyhole:

"SEVEN QUARTERS YOU'VE MADE ME WAIT!
SEVEN QUARTERS! NOW IT'S TOO LATE.
SO COMB AWAY FOR SEVEN YEARS MORE,
AND THEN GREAT DANGER LIES IN STORE.
YOU'LL COMB AWAY YOUR OWN CHILD'S BREATH;
YOU'LL COMB ROSEPETAL TO HER DEATH."

And with these angry words, the old woman disappeared. Rosalina took very little notice of them. She thought of nothing but her little Rosepetal who grew bigger and more delightful every day. Like her mother, she had remarkably long and lovely hair, and it was Rosalina's greatest pleasure to shut herself up in the secret room, alone with Rosepetal and comb it. The child grew to be almost seven years old, and the time was near when the old witch woman's curse was to come true:

"YOU'LL COMB AWAY YOUR OWN CHILD'S BREATH;
YOU'LL COMB ROSEPETAL TO HER DEATH."

But Rosalina did not think of that. She went on combing Rosepetal's hair, just as before.

Now one day, when she had the little girl clasped between her knees and was passing a golden comb through her long golden hair, she suddenly felt a great surge of envy, because the child's hair was so much prettier than her own, and she said crossly:

"I WISH THE HAIR WAS OFF YOUR HEAD, AND BRAIDED UP ON MINE INSTEAD!"

No sooner had she said these words, however, than punishment was sent from Heaven. Down came an invisible pair of scissors and cut all the hair off her head — snip, snap! She started in such amazement that her hand jerked, driving the sharp comb into poor Rosepetal's little head so hard that the child uttered a cry and fell down dead at her feet.

Then poor unhappy Rosalina remembered the old woman's magical curse, but it was too late now. There lay her beloved Rosepetal, dead upon the floor, and her own beautiful hair, of which she had been so vain and which she had combed so long, was all cut off and lay around her. She wrung her hands in despair over her shorn head.

She wept for a long time, and then she stuffed a little mattress with her long hair, filled a pillow with rose petals and laid dead Rosepetal on them with her hands folded, inside a coffin of crystal glass, with six more crystal coffins over it. Then she locked them all away in her secret chamber, which was known to no one but herself and one faithful serving maid.

So she lived on for several years, in constant mourning. The rosebush in her room withered away, and when she felt the hour of her death draw near she asked her brother, the Duke of Rosery, to come to her and told him, "Dear brother, the end of my life has come. I wish I had not been so willful and so vain, but it is too late to mend matters now,

and I pray to God to have mercy on me. All I owned is yours now. But promise me one thing, so that I can die in peace."

The Duke in tears, promised to do all she asked, for he loved her more than anything in the world.

So she gave him a key, saying, "This is the key to the innermost chamber of my apartments. Take great care of it, and never unlock that room."

Her brother assured her once again that he would keep his word.

"Farewell," said Rosalina, "and pray for me." Then she turned over and died, and the Duke had her buried with great pomp and ceremony beside the bush that bore the monthly roses.

A few months later, the Duke married a lady who was beautiful but ill-natured. One day he had to go away on a brief journey, and he asked his wife to look after the castle, warning her, whatever she did, not to unlock the innermost chamber, whose key he kept in his desk.

She promised to do as he said, but as soon as his back was turned curiosity drove her to fetch the key and open the forbidden chamber. When she saw Rosepetal lying on her mattress inside the glass coffins, she was consumed with fury! Ever since her mother had locked Rosepetal in the room, thinking she was dead, the child had been growing, and the glass coffins with her.

Now she looked like a lovely young girl of fourteen lying there asleep, for the old witch woman had kept her alive in her slumbers all these years.

Angrily, the wicked Duchess flung open the coffins. "Oho!" said she.

"So that's why I am not allowed into this room — so that this fine young lady here can sleep in peace! We'll soon see about that. I'll wake you, my sleeping beauty!" And she hauled Rosepetal's head up by the hair so roughly that the comb, which was still sticking in her head, fell out and the poor little girl awoke from her magical sleep, crying out, "Oh, Mother, dear Mother, how you hurt me!"

"I'll mother you and father you!" said the Duchess. "And I'll see you don't forget it either!" She pulled Rosepetal, weeping and trembling, out of her crystal coffin, and beat and ill-treated her in all kinds of ways, threatening to drown her if she ever breathed a word to anyone about what had happened to her in this room. Then she cut off the girl's beautiful long hair, gave her a short dress made of sacking, and forced her to fetch firewood and carry water, light the stoves and scour the rooms. She gave her so many blows and cuffs daily, boxing her ears and slapping her, that poor Rosepetal's face was all black and blue, as if she had been eating blueberries.

When the Duke of Rosery came home and asked his Duchess about the poor girl whom he saw her ill-treating so harshly every day, she said, "Oh, she's a slave girl my aunt sent me, but she is so vicious and stupid and lazy that I have to keep punishing her."

Well, after a while the Duke went away to a great fair, and according to his custom he summoned everyone who lived in the castle, down to the very cats and dogs, and asked them all what presents he should bring them home. One asked for this, another for that, and finally poor Rosepetal stepped forward too, in her coarse servant's dress. The Duke was about to speak to her when his wicked wife interrupted him.

"Must we have this dirty wench always about the place?" said she. "Are the rest of us to be put on a footing with this common, lazy slave girl? Send the wretched creature away! I don't know how you can show so low a wretch such honor!"

Tears of grief ran down poor Rosepetal's cheeks, and the kindhearted Duke was touched. "Don't cry, my poor child," he said. "Just say what you would like, for I intend to please you, and no one will stop me!" "Oh, sir," said Rosepetal, "bring me a doll, and a little knife and a whetstone, and if you forget, I wish you may not be able to cross the first river you come to on your way home."

So the Duke went off to the fair, and he bought everything else, but he forgot Rosepetal's doll and her little knife and whetstone.

On his way back he came to a river, and such a storm arose that no boatman dared ferry him over, and then he remembered Rosepetal's curse. He turned back at once and bought the things she wanted, and then he traveled home to his castle safe and sound, and gave all his presents.

Once Rosepetal had her own gifts she took them into the kitchen, put the doll upon the kitchen range, sat down in front of it, weeping bitterly, and began talking to it as if it were a living person, telling it all the torments she had to suffer at the Duchess's hands. "Do you hear me?" she kept saying. "Do you understand? Are you listening? Isn't it a sad story? What do you think?" But when the doll made no reply, Rosepetal took her little knife and sharpened it on her whetstone, saying, "Little doll, if you won't answer me I'll stab myself to the heart with this knife, for I have no friend on earth but you."

Then the doll began to swell up slowly, like bagpipes when the piper is blowing into them, and at last there was a whirring sound and words came out. "I understand, I understand, I hear, I hear, I understand."

Now the Duke had a room next door to the kitchen, and when he overheard the doll's song and Rosepetal's weeping and wailing several days running, he made a hole in the door so that he could see and hear Rosepetal sitting in front of her doll in tears, telling her story.

She told the tale of Prince Evermore and the pumpkin seeds, the festival of jumping the rose, the rose petal, the golden pumpkin that had been her cradle, her mother's combing of her hair, the witch woman's curse, the driving of the comb into her head, her enchanted sleep as she lay inside the seven glass coffins, the giving of the key to the Duke, who was forbidden to enter the chamber, the death of Princess Rosalina, the Duke's journey and the Duchess's curiosity, the unlocking of the forbidden chamber, the falling out of the comb, the cutting of her own hair, and the harsh treatment she had suffered every hour of the day.

Then she said, once again, "Answer me or I will kill myself!" And she set the point of the knife to her heart. But the Duke burst in through the doorway and snatched the knife from her hand. He embraced his niece lovingly, and took her out of the castle and away to the wife of his chief minister, who dressed her in fine clothes and cared for her well.

A few months later, when she had quite recovered from all her hard work and the ill-treatment given by the wicked Duchess, the Duke held a magnificent banquet in his castle and introduced Rosepetal as his niece. No one knew her in all her splendor. At the end of the meal a model of a house made of sugar was brought in, and everyone wanted to know what was inside it.

"Will you open the sugar house?" the Duke asked the Duchess.

So she opened it, and there was the little doll inside, lying in seven glass coffins just as Rosepetal had lain. The Duchess was afraid, and so angry that she broke the coffins open and snatched out the doll. But the doll ran away from her and perched on Rosepetal's shoulder, where she puffed herself up and up like a pair of bagpipes, and whirred, and spoke, accusing the Duchess of all her cruelties to her face.

And still the doll grew bigger and bigger, until at last, there on the table stood the old enchantress who has played many a part in this story. When she finished her speech, she flew away out of the window.

Then the Duke had his wicked wife put into a coach and driven back to her parents' house, where he had once gone to fetch her.

Rosepetal married a handsome prince, and had the whole dukedom of Rosery for her dowry, and the rosebush Evermore flowered again.

One night, as Rosepetal was breathing in its sweet scent, she and her husband went to the window, and she saw her mother and the braiding maids jumping over the rosebush, and Prince Evermore was also there.

"God bless you, dear Mother and Father!" she cried.

"God bless you, dear children!" they called up from down below, and then they vanished into thin air.

Then Rosepetal became very quiet and gentle in her ways. She had a cradle made, just like a golden pumpkin, and Heaven soon sent her a little prince to lay in the cradle, and he told me this tale for a piece of gingerbread I gave him.

Originally published in the United States, Canada, Great Britain, Australia, and
New Zealand in 1985 by Picture Book Studio. Reissued in 1995 by North-South Books,
an imprint of Nord-Süd Verlag AG, Gossau Zürich, Switzerland.

Distributed in the United States by North-South Books Inc., New York.

Library of Congress Cataloging-in-Publication Data
Brentano, Clemens, 1778-1842
The legend of rosepetal.
Translation of: Das Märchen von Rosenblättchen.
Summary: A lover of roses with most of her kingdom made into a rose garden,
Princess Rosalina makes a pact with an old enchantress to obtain the most beautiful
rosebush of all.
1. Children's stories, German. [1. Fairy tales] I. Zwerger, Lisbeth, ill. II. Title
PZ8.B674Le 1985 [E] 84-27386

A CIP catalogue record for this book is available from The British Library.

ISBN 1-55858-484-6
10 9 8 7 6 5 4 3 2 1
Printed in Italy

Ask your bookseller for these other North-South books illustrated by Lisbeth Zwerger:

DWARF NOSE by Wilhelm Hauff
LULLABIES, LYRICS AND GALLOWS SONGS by Christian Morgenstern
THE SWINEHERD by Hans Christian Andersen
LITTLE RED CAP by Jacob and Wilhelm Grimm
THE ART OF LISBETH ZWERGER, A Retrospective Catalog